MW00929408

THUNDER TRUCKS!

OFF-ROAD LEGENDS

BY BLAKE HOENA

ILLUSTRATED BY FERN CANO

Capstone Young Readers
a capstone imprint

ThunderTrucks! is published by
Stone Arch Books
a Capstone imprint
1710 Roe Crest Drive
North Mankato, Minnesota 56003
www.mycapstone.com

Copyright © 2018 by Capstone

All rights reserved. No part of this publication may be
reproduced in whole or in part, or stored in a retrieval
system, or transmitted in any form or by any means,
electronic, mechanical, photocopying, recording, or
otherwise, without written permission of the publisher.

Cataloging-in-Publication Data is available on the
Library of Congress website.

ISBN: 978-1-68436-038-3 (paperback)

Summary: Monster trucks combined with Greek myths
create legendary stories for early readers. From
Atalanta trying to prove she is the fastest truck in the
world to Odysseus facing off with Cyclopes and Achilles
in an epic competition, these stories will have readers
racing to finish.

Designed by Brann Garvey

Printed and bound in the United States
PA017

CONTENTS

COLOSSAL COURSE!

CHAPTER ONE

HERO WANTED

A small, rookie truck named B-phon rolls into Trolympia. It is his first visit to the capital.

"Wow! This city is huge," he honks.

All around him, trucks zoom through the streets. They honk excitedly. *HONK! HONK!* They beep loudly. *BEEP! BEEP!*

"What's all the excitement about?" B-phon asks.

The other trucks ignore him. They just zip on by.

VWOOOOSH!

"Where is everyone going?" B-phon tries to ask.

The streets are crowded, but not one truck pays him any attention. B-phon is simply a small truck in a big city.

Above him, he spots helicopters whirling about. They follow the crowd of trucks toward the center of the city.

If only I could fly, B-phon thinks. *I could see what is going on.*

B-phon watches as more and more trucks zoom down the street. Then he hears some truck beep, "Perseus is making a surprise visit!"

Perseus is a famous ThunderTruck. He raced Medusa in the World Endur-X Challenge.

Another truck honks, "I think Theseus is coming!"

Theseus challenged Bulltastic to race through the endless Monster Maze!

Then a truck asks, "Is Hercules going to be there too?"

Hercules was the first ThunderTruck to complete the Rough & Tough Twelve!

"Wow!" B-phon beeps. "My three favorite hero trucks!"

B-phon wants to be famous like Perseus, Theseus, and Hercules. They were the big three. He wishes he were half as famous as them—or even a teeny, tiny bit as famous.

B-phon also wishes he had a special power. All ThunderTrucks have one.

Perseus can leap higher and farther than any other truck. Theseus can outthink and outsmart all other trucks. Hercules is the mightiest truck on Earth!

But B-phon, all he knows how to do is get covered with dust and mud.

As trucks speed by, they splatter B-phon with mud. They kick up clouds of dust that cause him to choke and cough.

"I want — **COUGH! COUGH!** — to go to — **COUGH! COUGH!**" he coughs.

B-phon joins the crowd. He follows the other trucks as they stream into the pit. It is a huge monster truck arena in the center of the city. Trucks fill up the stands.

On the track below, B-phon spots Perseus and Theseus.

Trucks beep, **"Perseus! Perseus!"**

Trucks honk, **"Theseus! Theseus!"**

"Where is Hercules?" some trucks ask.

Slowly, the rumbles become louder than the beeps and honks.

"Hercules needs a tune up after completing the Rough & Tough Twelve," Perseus says.

"So he won't be joining us today," Theseus adds.

The rumbles turn to disappointed sighs.

"But we have exciting news!" Perseus continues.

"One of you can join us on an adventure!" Theseus adds.

All the trucks in the stands get quiet.

"We have been challenged to a race by the Chimera Brothers," Perseus says.

B-phon has heard of the Chimera Brothers monster trucks. One is called The Goat and another The Lion. The last one is The Dragon. They are some of the scariest monster trucks around. They have turned everyone they have raced into rust buckets!

"There are three of them and only two of us," Theseus adds.

B-phon hears a rumble in the crowd.

"We will face The Goat," Perseus says. "He can ram a truck hard enough to knock all four tires off with one blow."

"We will face The Lion," Theseus says.

"With his spiked bumpers, he can tear

your fenders off."

"Lastly is The Dragon," Perseus says.
"He shoots flames from his grill!"

"If you survive getting rammed by The
Goat and The Lion," Theseus says. "The
Dragon will fry you!"

B-phon can barely hear the heroes
speak with the engines revving and tires
screeching all around him.

"Who would like to face the Chimera

Brothers with us?" Perseus asks.

Silence.

B-phon looks around. He is alone in

the stands.

"You're our third

racer!" Theseus

shouts to B-phon.

CHAPTER TWO

PERSEUS GETS PUMMELED

The next day, B-phon rolls out of Trolympia with the two famous heroes.

"I can't believe it," he says. "I'm going on an adventure!"

Perseus and Theseus look at each other.

"Will there be danger?" B-phon asks. "Will we risk bumper and fender?"

B-phon is excited. He can't stop talking. Perseus and Theseus both sigh.

"Have you raced the Chimera Brothers before?" he asks. "Which one scares you the most?"

He does not get an answer. The heroes speed ahead. They ignore B-phon and talk about their past adventures.

"Remember that time we raced against Jason?" Perseus says.

"I can't believe he won the Golden Fenders," Theseus replies.

As the heroes relive past adventures, B-phon worries about this adventure.

Many trucks have taken up the Chimera Brothers' challenge. Most of them were turned to heaps of scrap.

"Do we have a plan?" B-phon asks. "How can we beat the Chimera Brothers?"

SCREEECH! The two heroes skid to a halt. They glance back at B-phon.

"Everything will be fine," Perseus says.

"We're ThunderTrucks, and ThunderTrucks always win," Theseus adds.

Then they turn and continue on.

"How much farther?" B-phon asks. "Wouldn't it be quicker if we could fly there?"

The ThunderTrucks ignore him as they climb up a hill. Below is the Chimera Brothers' racetrack. It is filled with obstacles, from mud pits to jumps over smashed wrecks and steep berms.

"Wow!" B-phon says. "That looks dangerous. Doesn't that look dangerous?"

Perseus and Theseus don't reply. They head down the other side of the hill.

"Here they come," The Lion roars.

"Who's with them?" The Goat bleats.

"Doesn't matter," The Dragon snorts. "He's toast!"

B-phon and the two ThunderTrucks roll up to the evil monster trucks.

"Remember what we are racing for?" The Lion asks.

"Winners get the losers' engines," Theseus says.

"After we are through with you," The Goat begins.

"You will never race again," The Dragon finishes with a snort.

B-phon gulps. He saved up all of his allowance just to buy his Soarin' V6 engine. He doesn't want to risk losing it. But it's too late to back out now.

"Every truck get ready!" an official suddenly blares.

B-phon rolls up to the starting line
with the other trucks.

"Set!"

Engines rev.

"GO!"

Tires spin,
kicking up dirt.

The Dragon shoots a blast of fire at
B-phon. He swerves to avoid it and spins off
the track.

In last place, B-phon watches Theseus
speed off, taking the lead.

Then he sees The Lion nipping at Perseus'
tires. Perseus tries to leap out of the way. As
he does, The Goat rams into him.

Perseus lands on his side in the middle of the track with a loud **THUD!**

The Dragon rolls up to Perseus. He is about to roast Perseus!

CHAPTER THREE

THESEUS GETS THUMPED

"Noooooo!" B-phon screams.

He jumps back onto the track. With dust flying, he speeds toward Perseus. B-phon swerves into The Dragon with a **THUMP!** as the monster lets loose a blast of flame. It blackens the ground beside Perseus.

As the Chimera Brothers race after Theseus, B-phon pushes Perseus onto his tires.

"You saved me," Perseus says.

"Can you continue the race?" B-phon asks.

Perseus sputters, limping badly.

"I think I cracked an axle," he says. "You need to go help Theseus."

"But how?" B-phon asks. "I'm not a ThunderTruck. I don't even have a special power."

"Every truck has a special power," Perseus says. "Now go!"

B-phon rejoins the race as Perseus limps off the track.

B-phon speeds over jumps. He bucks and spins through a mud pit. He darts around spike-covered barriers.

Up ahead, he sees the Chimera Brothers. B-phon is catching up to them. But something is odd. They aren't going very fast.

Then Theseus races up behind him. **"I'm lapping you!"** he shouts as he zooms by B-phon.

Then B-phon understands what is happening. The Chimera Brothers aren't trying to catch up to Theseus. They are waiting to ambush him.

"Stop!" B-phon shouts.

But Theseus speeds away. He jumps over ramps. He spins through mud pits. He darts around spiked obstacles.

B-phon races after Theseus. But he is not quick enough to catch the ThunderTruck.

B-phon watches as Theseus darts by The Dragon. He easily passes The Lion. But when he tries to get by The Goat, The Goat cuts him off.

Theseus swerves to avoid crashing into The Goat. As he does, The Lion sneaks up behind him. He nips at Theseus' back tires with his spiked front bumper.

POP!

    POP!

POP!

Theseus' tires explode. He spins out in the middle of the track.

The Goat stops and turns around. He revs

his engine. His tires spin. Then he charges

Theseus. *VROOOOOOM!*

CRACK!

"Ooh! Ow! Oh. Ouch!"

Theseus groans as he tumbles down

the track. He lands on his side.

The Dragon rolls up to him. He revs his

engine and smoke pours out from his hood.

Theseus is about to get **fried!**

B-phon speeds forward as fast as he

can. As The Dragon starts to shoot flames,

B-phon bumps into him. The Dragon misses

and scorches the ground next the Theseus.

"You are toast," The Dragon snarls at B-phon. Then he races off.

B-phon rolls up to Theseus. He nudges the hero's tires.

"Are you okay?" B-phon asks.

"I don't think so," he sputters. Smoke pours out from under his hood. "I think I popped a piston or two."

B-phon pushes Theseus off the track.

"It is up to you to win this race," Theseus says.

"But I'm not a ThunderTruck!" B-phon says. "And I told you, I don't even have a special power."

"Yes, you do, B-phon," Theseus says.

"You just haven't needed it yet. Now go

win this thing!"

B-phon speeds off, determined to win.

CHAPTER FOUR

THREE ON ONE

B-phon now has two goals. One: He has to win the race. Two: He has to survive.

Surviving is probably more important and more difficult. But if he loses, he more than loses. The Chimera Brothers get his engine. A truck can't do much—or anything, really—without one.

B-phon revs his engine. His tires spin. Dirt flies. He races after the Chimera Brothers. He leaps over jumps. He zooms over berms.

But the brothers don't appear to be racing. They putter along the track, and B-phon easily catches up to them.

Then they stop, blocking his path.

"Hey, it's the hero wannabe," The Goat bleats.

"Careful or you might get hurt," The Lion roars.

"Or burnt to a crisp!" The Dragon snorts.

B-phon is not sure what to do. The brothers are in his way. And he saw what happened to Theseus when he tried to pass them.

The Goat charges. B-phon darts to the side. The Goat clips his back fender.

Next The Lion pounces. B-phon darts to the other side. The Lion scratches the other side of the back fender.

B-phon is left facing The Dragon. Smoke pours out from under his hood. B-phon knows what's coming next. But instead of running away from The Dragon, he charges and shoots up a ramp.

B-phon soars over the flames. But his underside gets a little scorched.

He lands on the other side of The Dragon with a **THUMP!**

Suddenly, B-phon finds himself in the lead. But now the three Chimera Brothers are really mad.

"He got away from us!" The Goat bleats.

"We can't let him win!" The Lion roars.

"It is **SUPER MONSTER** time!" The Dragon snorts.

What is Super Monster time? B-phon wonders.

He glances back, and what he sees scares him. As the Chimera Brothers race after B-phon, they join together. First The Goat rams into The Lion. Then The Dragon rams into The Goat and The Lion.

Their parts jumble together. The three monster trucks suddenly become one Super Monster Truck!

The Super Monster has spiked bumpers like The Lion. It has ramming horns like The Goat. It shoots flames from its grill like The Dragon. The Super Monster is three times as big and twice as fast, and it is catching up to B-phon.

CHAPTER FIVE

FLYING HIGH

"I could use a superpower right about now," B-phon mutters to himself.

The Super Monster is hot on his bumper. B-phon can feel his fiery breath. He can see his ramming horns getting closer. And he worries about the Super Monster's spiked bumpers too.

B-phon cannot outrace the Super Monster. So he slams on his brakes and skids to a stop. The Super Monster zips past. He does a 180 in the middle of the track to face B-phon.

"You are scrap," he rumbles.

His engine roars and his tires spins. The Super Monster speeds toward B-phon. Not knowing what else to do, B-phon rushes at him.

B-phon hopes to dart past the large truck. But as he veers to the right, Super Monster tries to cut him off. B-phon is forced up and over a berm. He expects to crash off the track.

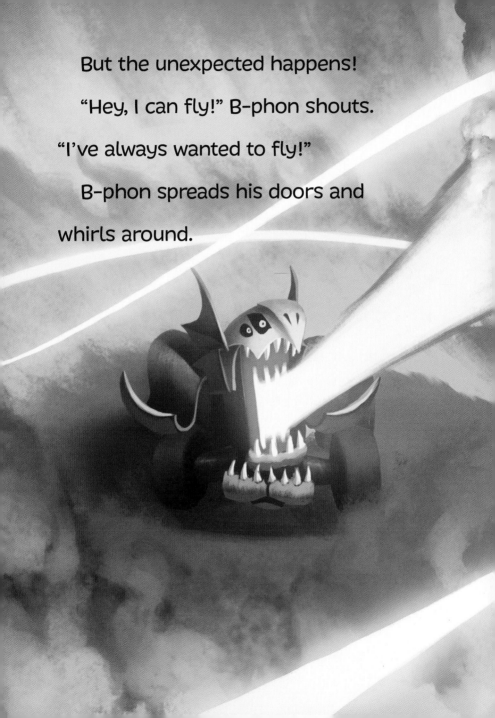

But the unexpected happens!

"Hey, I can fly!" B-phon shouts.

"I've always wanted to fly!"

B-phon spreads his doors and whirls around.

The Super Monster shoots flames at him.

But B-phon ducks and dives out of the way.

Then he swoops and spins around the

Super Monster. All the while, the bigger

truck tries to fry him.

Soon everything around the Super

Monster is on fire.

"Hey, I'm trapped!" it cries.

Then it starts to shake in fear. It shakes so hard that it falls apart, and the Chimera Brothers fall to the ground.

B-phon glides down the track. He speeds toward the finish line. The ref truck waves the checkered flag.

Suddenly, B-phon is surrounded by three hero trucks. Hercules is with Perseus and Theseus.

"You did it!" Perseus shouts.

"You're a hero!" Theseus shouts.

"Sorry I'm late," Hercules says. "But it looks like you didn't need me."

From down the track, they hear loud coughing and sputtering. The three Chimera Brothers limp and wheeze toward the finish line. Their tires are flat. Smoke pours out of their engines. And they are covered in black scorch marks.

"You won the race," Perseus says.

"You can take their engines," Theseus adds.

"Nah, I think I'll keep my Soarin' V6," B-phon says.

Just then, all four of The Goat's tires fall off. He lands on the ground with a **THUMP!** All of The Lion's fenders rattle to the ground. Then The Dragon crumples to a pile of ash.

"Look who's toast now!" B-phon says

with a laugh.

CHAPTER 1

THUNDERTRUCK XTREME RALLY

Excited trucks fill up the stands. They honk and beep as they cheer on their favorite ThunderTrucks.

An official hooks one end of a chain to Hercules' bumper. She hooks the other end to Theseus' bumper. A mud pit sits between the two rivals.

The Tug-o-War Championship
at the ThunderTruck
Xtreme Rally is about
to begin!

"You won't beat me
this time!" Hercules

shouts.

"We'll see about that,"
Theseus rumbles.

"Competitors, get
ready," the official blares.

The chain between Hercules and
Theseus snaps tight. *TCHING!*

"Get set!"

The ThunderTrucks rev their engines.

VROOM! VROOM!

"Pull!"

Tires screech. Dirt

flies. Engines roar.

Theseus jerks forward.

He drags Hercules, tires spinning,

toward the pit.

Mud bubbles up and splashes the

mighty ThunderTruck.

"Eat mud!" Theseus yells.

At the edge of the pit, the treads of

Hercules' tires dig in.

"Not this time," Hercules shouts. His engine rumbles. **RUMBLE! RUMBLE!** He tugs and yanks and jerks. Inch by inch, he drags Theseus toward the pit.

Theseus' tires spin. His engine whines. He kicks up a cloud of dirt. But nothing can stop the mighty Hercules.

Theseus lands in the pit with a SPLASH! Oozing mud covers him from tailpipe to windshield.

"Looks like you need to hit the car wash!" Hercules laughs.

Other ThunderTrucks rush over to congratulate Hercules.

"Wow, I thought Theseus was going win," Atalanta says.

"Great match, Hercules!" Perseus says.

Hercules just puffs out a cloud of exhaust and rolls away. Theseus crawls out of the mud pit and heads in another direction.

* * *

The next competition at the ThunderTruck Xtreme Rally is about to start. Hercules rolls up in front of a ramp. Beyond is a row of flaming tires. He revs his engine. *VROOM!* *VROOM!* Then he takes off in a cloud of dust.

Hercules hits the ramp and leaps into the air. He flies over 10 . . . 20 . . . 30 . . . 40 . . . 47 flaming tires!

The crowd beeps, "Hercules! Hercules!"

As Hercules drives by Theseus, he honks, "Beat that!"

Theseus looks at the flags atop the stadium. They flutter in the wind. Theseus waits until they point away from him. With the wind at his back, he is off. He hits the ramp. He sails over 10 . . . 20 . . . 30 . . . 40 . . . 50 . . . 52 flaming tires!

The crowd beeps, "Theseus! Theseus!"

"Yeah!" he shouts. "I won!"

Other ThunderTrucks rush over to congratulate Theseus.

"I didn't think you could beat Hercules' jump," B-phon says.

"That was incredible, Theseus," Argonutz says.

Theseus just puffs out a cloud of exhaust and rolls away. Hercules leaves in another direction. The rest of the ThunderTrucks are confused.

"What is wrong with those two?" Atalanta asks.

"They are getting way too competitive," Odysseus says.

At the next competition, things only get worse. Theseus and Hercules face off at a starting line.

"I am the best ThunderTruck there is!" Theseus roars.

"No, I am the World's Mightiest Truck!" Hercules rumbles. "I even have a decal that says so."

"Anyone can buy one of those at Royal Rumbler's Decal Shop," Theseus backfires.

The other ThunderTrucks drive between the two.

"Stop it!" Perseus says. "You two are supposed to be friends."

No one can believe that the two friends are arguing so much.

"We need a contest to decide who is the best!" Hercules beeps. "Like completing the Rough & Tough Twelve."

"Or racing through the Monster Maze," Theseus honks.

The two ThunderTrucks honk and beep at each other. Then a mysterious MonsterTruck rolls over. It is black with tinted windows.

"You need something more challenging," the truck says in a raspy voice.

"What do you have in mind?" Hercules beeps.

"I challenge you to race through the Underworld," the truck says.

Theseus and Hercules look at each other

"I'm in!" Hercules rumbles.

"Me too," Theseus blares.

The other ThunderTrucks gasp in shock. Only trucks that cannot be repaired go to the Underworld.

None of them have ever returned.

CHAPTER 2

THE RIVER STICKY

The next day, Hercules and Theseus meet in front of a large iron cave. A neon sign above the entrance flashes the word "Underworld."

A stream of trucks rolls through the gate. They are run-down rust buckets. Some putter along. Others sputter and cough out puffs of smoke. Some are dented. Others limp along on broken axles and flat tires. None look repairable.

The black MonsterTruck rolls up to

Hercules and Theseus.

"Many enter the Underworld," the

MonsterTruck says. "None have returned."

Theseus and Hercules look at each other.

"That's about to change," Hercules rumbles.

"Yeah, because I will be the first!" Theseus shouts.

"Then get ready," the dark truck says.

Theseus and Hercules roll up to the edge of the cave. Both look determined.

"Get set!"

The two ThunderTrucks rev their engines. ***VROOM! VROOM!***

"Go!"

Tires spin and dirt flies as Hercules and Theseus take off.

ZOOM! They dart through the entrance and into the Underworld. Inside is a dark and rocky tunnel. It twists and turns as it slopes down into blackness.

Both of the ThunderTrucks flick on their headlights. They weave in and out of the rust buckets. They speed through the tunnel.

First Theseus takes the lead. "Ha! I'm winning," he honks.

Then Hercules darts in front. "I'm gonna win!" he beeps.

Suddenly the tunnel opens up into a large cavern. Hundreds of beat-up trucks sputter along. They head toward a bridge that crosses a dark, oily river.

Theseus and Hercules try to weave through the other trucks. But there are too many of them. They come screeching to a halt in the world's largest traffic jam. The dark MonsterTruck rolls up to them.

"This is your first challenge," he says.

"Whoa, you scared me," Hercules beeps in surprise.

"Where did you come from?" Theseus asks.

The MonsterTruck does not answer.

"That is the River Sticky," he says. "The only way across is the toll bridge."

All the trucks head toward a narrow, rickety bridge. One at a time, they roll up to a gate and put a coin in the slot. The gate rises, and then they slowly cross.

"It will take years to get through this traffic jam," Hercules grumbles.

"There has to be another way around,"
Theseus says. "Come on."

The two trucks turn away from the
bridge. They race along the banks of the
River Sticky.

"It's too far to jump across," Hercules
says. "Even for Perseus."

Every ThunderTruck has a special
ability. Perseus can jump father than
any other truck. Theseus is one of the
smartest trucks around. He has an idea.

"Follow me," he beeps.

Up ahead is a steep cliff. The River
Sticky flows from a dark tunnel in its
rocky wall.

Theseus sees a rusty van stuck in the muck at the edge of the river. He races up to it and uses the rust bucket as a ramp.

Theseus sails into the air. He twists and lands with all four tires on the wall. He races across the cliff and leaps.

When he reaches the other side of the river, he turns to see if Hercules followed him.

THUD!

The mighty ThunderTruck lands next to Theseus.

"Good thinking," Hercules says. "But now the race is back on!"

He darts off, leaving Theseus in a cloud of dust. Theseus speeds after him.

CHAPTER 3

THE MUTT

The ThunderTrucks race along the opposite shore of the River Sticky. Hercules is in the lead. But Theseus is nipping at his mud flaps.

Then the mighty Hercules slams on his brakes. **SCRRREEECH!**

He skids to a stop in front of a narrow tunnel. A stream of dented and rusty trucks enters the tunnel.

Theseus slides up to Hercules. "Why did you stop?" Theseus asks. "We can go around them."

"But I don't think we can get around him," Hercules says.

A truck rolls out of the shadows. It is huge! It looks as if it were built out of the spare parts of other trucks. It blocks their way.

Just then, the black truck rolls up to them. "That is The Mutt," the black truck says in his raspy voice.

"Stop sneaking up on us!" Hercules honks.

"Yeah, who do you think you are?" Theseus asks.

The MonsterTruck does not answer. He just looks ahead.

"The Mutt is your next challenge," he says.

"How do we get past him?" Theseus asks.

"I got this," Hercules rumbles.

Hercules also has a talent. He is the strongest of all ThunderTrucks. He revs his engine **VROOM! VROOM!** as he rolls up to The Mutt.

"Only junkers can pass," The Mutt growls.

"Who's going to stop me!" Hercules rumbles.

The two trucks go bumper to bumper. Hercules revs his engine. **VROOM! VROOM!** He pushes The Mutt back.

Then The Mutt's engine roars. **RRR! RRR!** He shoves Hercules back toward the River Sticky.

Back and forth they push and shove. Their engines roar. **RRR! RRR!** Their tires spin and squeal. A cloud of dust surrounds them.

As they battle, Theseus sees his chance. He sneaks by The Mutt and into the tunnel.

Theseus is almost to the other side of the tunnel when he looks back. Theseus can see that Hercules is exhausted. Puffs of smoke pour out from under his hood, and he has one flat tire. Theseus knows that soon Hercules will bust a piston.

Theseus sneaks up behind The Mutt. He hooks his winch to The Mutt's back bumper. When Hercules revs his engine to give a mighty push, Theseus revs his engine too.

VROOM! VROOM! He tugs and pulls The Mutt backward. This gives Hercules time to dart around the MonsterTruck.

CHAPTER 4

THE JUNKYARD

The MonsterTruck waits for Theseus and Hercules at the other end of the tunnel. Scaring them again.

"You are creeping me out!" Hercules honks.

"How did you get past The Mutt?" Theseus asks.

But the strange truck ignores them. Instead, he turns to show the ThunderTrucks what is ahead of them.

The tunnel opens up into a huge cave. Junky trucks litter its floor.

"This is The Junkyard. Crossing it is your next challenge," the MonsterTruck says. "Good luck!"

The two ThunderTrucks set off. They zigzag between trucks. They jump over dunes. They race bumper to bumper.

"I don't see what is so hard about this," Hercules beeps.

But just then, Theseus jerks to a stop.

"Ow!" Theseus beeps. "Something yanked on my back bumper."

Hercules glances back. A rusty tow truck has hooked on to Theseus.

"Let go of my friend!" Hercules blares.

But then he sees something that scares him. All the junked-out trucks are coming to life.

Slowly, the wrecks rise and chug their way toward the two ThunderTrucks.

"This isn't good," Theseus beeps. "What will we do?"

"Grab on!" Hercules honks.

Theseus hooks his winch's cable up to Hercules. Then the World's Mightiest ThunderTruck gives a mighty tug. He breaks Theseus free of the old tow truck.

"We are surrounded," Theseus beeps.

"Not for long!" Hercules blares.

Hercules darts forward, pulling Theseus. Then he spins a 360. Theseus sails through the air at the end of the winch's cable.

Hercules holds on to the other end of the cable. His friend flies around in a big circle.

As Theseus whips about, he **SMASHES** and **CRASHES** and **BASHES** through the wrecks surrounding them. Then he swings around and lands next to Hercules.

"Whoa!" Theseus says. "That was amazing!"

"But we aren't out of here yet," Hercules beeps.

As the pair watch, more and more junkers sputter and chug toward them.

They speed off. But they are still in the middle of The Junkyard and facing hundreds of rust buckets.

"It's Demolition Derby time!" the ThunderTrucks beep.

Hercules crashes into a junker, knocking off its fenders.

Theseus flies over a dune. He lands on a rust bucket and flattens it.

Hercules drives over wreck after wreck, crushing them beneath his tires.

Theseus pinballs from junker to junker, scattering trucks left and right.

The pair **SMASHES** and **CRASHES**
and **BASHES** their way through the
Underworld.

Spare parts litter the path behind them.

Then they leave The Junkyard behind.

CHAPTER 5

KING OF THE SCRAP HEAP

Hercules and Theseus continue on, but they are no longer racing. Instead, they drive side by side.

"This has been fun," Hercules says.

"Yeah, but we aren't out of the Underworld yet," Theseus says. "Look!"

Up ahead is a huge pile of old trucks. A black truck sits on top of the big heap.

"What are you doing here?"

Theseus asks.

"And where is the exit?"

Hercules asks.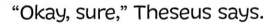

"Don't you want to

know who I am first?" the

MonsterTruck asks.

"Okay, sure," Theseus says.

 "As long as you tell us

how to get out of here,"

Hercules says.

The truck looks from

Theseus to Hercules. Then

he takes a deep breath.

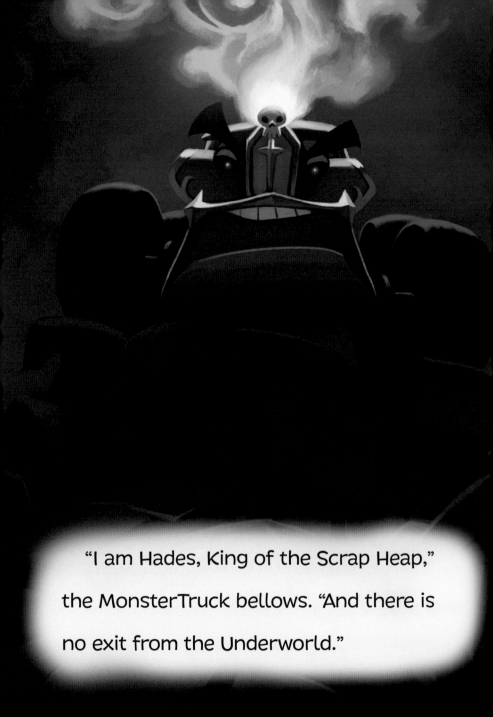

"I am Hades, King of the Scrap Heap," the MonsterTruck bellows. "And there is no exit from the Underworld."

Theseus and Hercules glance at each other.

"Then let's make one!" they shout.

Hercules' engine roars. **RRR! RRR!**

Theseus revs up his engine. **_VROOM!_**
VROOM.

Their tires spin and squeal as they take off. They race toward the scrap heap.

"What are you doing?" Hades asks. But the ThunderTrucks don't answer.

When they get to the scrap heap, they race up it.

RRR! RRR! Hercules picks up speed.
VROOM! VROOM! Theseus goes faster and faster.

When they reach the top, they are just a blur.

"Stop!" Hades shouts.

Too late! The ThunderTrucks smash into him. They knock him off the scrap heap. Hades falls and lands with a huge **THUD!**

But Hercules and Theseus do not stop. They use the large pile of junk as a giant ramp. At the top, they fly up into the air. Their speed carries them toward the ceiling of the Underworld.

Then **BOOM!** Together, they crash through the ceiling.

An explosion of dirt and rocks startles a group of ThunderTrucks.

When the dust clears, Theseus and Hercules stand proudly among their friends.

"You're back," Atalanta beeps.

"So who won?" B-phon asks.

"We both did—as a team!" Theseus honks.

"We are the first to escape the Underworld!" Hercules blares.

The other ThunderTrucks congratulate them.

"Come celebrate with us," Perseus says.

"We're heading to the Spare Parts Buffet for a snack," Odysseus adds.

"I am starving," Hercules says.

"Bet I can eat more oil-covered bolts than you," Theseus said.

"Can not!" Hercules rumbles.

"Those two are like a couple of spare tires," Argonutz says.

"They never change," Atalanta adds.

CHAPTER ONE

SUPER SPRINT

"Racers, get ready!" a race official blares.

Atalanta rolls up to the starting line. She revs her engine.

To her right is the mighty Hercules. His engine roars.

RRRR! RRRR!

On her left is Perseus with his winged-shaped mud flaps. His engine rumbles.

RUMBLE! RUMBLE!

The other ThunderTrucks—Theseus, B-phon, Argonutz, and Odysseus—roll up to the starting line together.

Hercules is the World's Mightiest Truck. He even has a decal that says so.

At the ThunderJam 3000, Perseus jumped over an amazing 90 flaming tires.

Theseus is the only ThunderTruck smart enough to solve the Monster Maze.

Atalanta has a special skill too. She is the speediest of them all. At least that is what she hopes to prove at the ThunderTruck Super Sprint.

"Get set!" the official blares.

Engines rev, roar, and rumble even louder.

VROOM! RRRR! RUMBLE!

"GO!" the official blares.

Tires spin. Dust flies. The crowd *HONKS!* and *BEEPS!* as the race begins.

Atalanta zips into the lead. The mighty Hercules quickly falls behind. Even Theseus, Argonutz, and Odysseus cannot keep up. They are all left in Atalanta's dust.

As the racers round a turn, Perseus zooms up a small hill. He leaps high into the air. He lands with a *THUD* next to Atalanta.

"You really are fast," Perseus says with a gasp. He tries to keep pace.

"You haven't seen anything yet!" Atalanta beeps.

Her tires *SQUEAL*, and she darts ahead of Perseus.

B-phon opens his doors. They spread
out wide like wings. *WHOOSH!*
He takes flight and soars into the air.

Atalanta looks up as he starts to
catch her.

"You won't pass
me," Atalanta beeps.

Her engine whines.
She dashes ahead of
B-phon.

Atalanta darts around the track faster
than any other ThunderTruck. She sails
over jumps and zips around turns. She
zooms down the straightaways.

Up ahead, the official waves a
checkered flag. Atalanta speeds across
the finish line and **SCREEEECHES**
to a stop.

The crowd cheers, "Atalanta! Atalanta!"

The other trucks pass the finish line.

"Wow!" Perseus beeps.

"You are really fast,"

Theseus says.

"I bet we can find you a sticker

that says

'World's Speediest

Truck,'" Hercules adds.

"I bet she's not,"

a loud voice says.

Suddenly, the crowd goes silent.

A giant, flame-red truck rolls up to the group of ThunderTrucks. A cloud of smoke puffs above him.

"Bullistic!" the audience gasps. "It's Bullistic!"

"You aren't the World's Speediest Truck until you beat me," Bullistic booms. "And that won't happen!"

"I am not afraid to race you," Atalanta says.

"Then I challenge you to a race through the Monster Maze!" Bullistic bellows. "Tomorrow. Be there."

And with that, Bullistic puffs away.

CHAPTER 2

MONSTER MAZE

The next day, Atalanta meets Theseus before the race. He is the only ThunderTruck to ever beat Bullistic.

The Monster Maze is a course full of twists and turns through a dark canyon.

"I brought this to help you," Theseus says.

He sets down a silver winch.

"What's that for?" Atalanta beeps.

"I used it to find my way out of the maze," Theseus says. "Before you enter, hook the cable to a tree near the entrance."

Atalanta puts the winch on her back bumper. She hooks its cable to the tree. Then she goes to face Bullistic.

"The rules are simple," a race official says. "First one to the center of the maze and back wins."

"Got it," Atalanta beeps.

"Racers, get ready," the official blares.

Atalanta revs her engine.

VROOM! VROOM!

"Get set!" the official yells.

SNNNOOORRRTTT! Bullistic zooms

off into the maze before the official

even says go!

Atalanta races after him. The cable from the winch trails behind her.

Within the maze, rocky walls tower over her. They block out all but a sliver of sunlight. Soon, Atalanta is lost in the twisting and winding of the tunnels.

"Ugh! Another dead end!" Atalanta honks.

She speeds down a canyon and wheels around a turn. She screeches to a halt as she comes grill-to-grill with a rocky cliff.

"Again!" she honks.

Twist after turn, Atalanta makes her way through the maze.

The narrow path she raced down opens up into a large cavern. Ahead, the road suddenly disappears. Atalanta **SCREECHES** to a stop at the edge of another cliff.

"Whoa! That was close," she beeps.

Below are sharp, jagged rocks. Atalanta also sees junked trucks at the bottom of the pit.

Then a large, dark shadow moves over her. She spins around to see Bullistic blocking the path.

"Congrats," he snorts. "You have found the middle of the maze."

"Now I just need to find the exit," Atalanta beeps.

"Not going to happen," Bullistic snorts. "You're about to join the rest of my competitors in the pit."

Bullistic's engine roars.

RRRR! RRRR! RRRR!

His tires **SQUEAL!** as he charges. Atalanta winds the winch's cable around a rock.

When Bullistic leaps forward, she darts to the side. The giant truck trips over the cable.

"AHHHHH!" he screams as he falls into the pit.

BOOM! He lands with a crash.

"Ow! My axle!" Bullistic groans.

"Time to go!" Atalanta beeps.

She follows the cable. She darts down tunnels until she reaches the entrance.

"Atalanta, you did it!" Theseus honks.

"You are the World's Speediest Truck!" Perseus honks.

Just then, a run down gas-guzzler sputters up to them.

"Medusa!" Atalanta beeps. "What do you want?"

"You aren't the World's Speediest Truck until you beat me," Medusa rattles. "I challenge you to a race in the Endur-X Championship. Tomorrow. Be there."

CHAPTER 3

ENDUR-X CHAMPIONSHIP

The next day, Atalanta meets Perseus at the Endur-X course. He is the only ThunderTruck to beat Medusa.

With just a bump, Medusa can turn any truck into a pile of scrap.

"You also need to be careful of her sisters, the Gorgonaters," Perseus warns. "They will try to cheat to help her win."

"Where are they?" Atalanta asks.

Perseus looks up to the  sky. "I don't know, but I know that they can fly."

"Racers, get ready!" the race official yells.

Atalanta rolls up to the starting line. She stays far away from Medusa.

"Get set!" the official says.

Atalanta revs her engine.

VROOM! VROOM!

Medusa sputters.

"GO!" the official yells.

Atalanta speeds away.

Atalanta looks back as she reaches the first part of the race, Mount Trolympus. She has left Medusa in her dust.

She starts her climb through a narrow canyon. Near the top, a large shadow crosses Atalanta's path.

She looks up just in time to see a boulder dropping from the sky.

SCRRREEECCCHHH! She stops.

BOOM! The large rock crashes right in front of her.

"It must be the Gorgonaters," Atalanta rumbles.

She continues up and over the mountain. On the other side is the Bottomless Bog.

Atalanta sets off slowly down a narrow and twisting path. She does not want to slip off and fall into the bubbling, oily bog.

As she slowly zigs and zags down the trail, another shadow passes over her. She looks up to see the Gorgonaters.

They are carrying Medusa over the bog. They set their sister down at the end of the path.

Cheaters never win! Atalanta thinks.

Now Atalanta's way is blocked, but
she is not going to let that stop her.
She revs her engine to build up speed.
VROOM! VROOM!
Then she turns off the path. She
is racing so fast, she skips across the
surface of the oily bog.

The Gorgonaters swoop down to stop her.

"We've got you now!" they scream.

Atalanta spins in a full circle and sprays bubbling oil everywhere. It splatters the Gorgonaters, and they crash into the bog. **SPLISH! SPLASH!**

Atalanta races on. She zooms across an endless desert, jumping over dunes and kicking up sand. She leaves Medusa, chugging and sputtering, far behind her.

She races until the ground drops away on both sides of the path. The thinning path leads to a narrow point.

Atalanta rolls up to the edge of a steep cliff. This is the end of the world!

"I made it!" Atalanta honks.

Then she zips back across the endless desert. She winds her way through the Bottomless Bog. She races up and over Mount Trolympus.

The ThunderTrucks wait for her on the other side.

"You did it!" Argonutz blares.

"You won another race!" B-phon honks.

As they are celebrating, three tough-looking trucks roll up to them.

It is the evil Chimera Brothers.

"She is not the World's Speediest Truck," The Goat bleats.

"Not unless she can beat us!" The Lion roars.

"On our Colossal Course!" The Dragon bellows as flames shoot out from his grill.

CHAPTER 4
COLOSSAL COURSE

The next day, Atalanta meets B-phon at the course. He is the only ThunderTruck to beat the Chimera Brothers. The course is filled with mud pits to sky-high jumps and steep berms.

"The Chimera Brothers will team up on you," B-phon warns. "First, The Lion will pop your tires. Then, The Goat will ram you, to knock you over. That's when The Dragon will fry you with his fire."

"Okay, got it," Atalanta beeps.

She rolls up to the starting line with the three MonsterTrucks.

"Racers, get ready!" the official blares.

Atalanta revs her engine.

"Get set!"

The Chimera Brothers' engines roar and rumble. **RRRR! RUMBLE!**

"Go!"

Tires spin, and the racers are off.

The Dragon shoots a blast of fire from his grill. Atalanta zigs to the right. The Goat turns to ram into her. Atalanta zags to the left.

The Lion nips at her heels. Atalanta puts the pedal to the metal, and she speeds ahead.

Atalanta zips around a turn. She hits a jump and sails over a pile of wrecks. She dives through mud pits and speeds down straightaways.

She is winning! But the Chimera
Brothers are not really racing. They are
waiting for Atalanta to come around and
lap them.

First, she zigs around The Dragon. He tries to blast her with fire.

Next, she zags around The Goat. He attempts to ram her.

Then, she darts past The Lion. He nips at her tires.

"This isn't working!" The Dragon bellows.

"She's too fast!" The Lion roars.

"It is Super Monster time!" The Goat bleats.

Atalanta looks back. What she sees causes her to race faster. The Chimera Brothers are ramming into one other.

Their parts jumble together until the three MonsterTrucks become one Super MonsterTruck.

"B-phon didn't warn me about this," Atalanta gasps.

The Super MonsterTruck is huge. It has spiked bumpers like The Lion. It has  ramming horns like The Goat and a flaming grill like The Dragon. It is now twice as fast and is quickly catching up to Atalanta.

"If ever I needed to be the speediest truck in the world," Atalanta beeps, "it is right now."

Blasts of fire melt her mud flaps. Spiked bumpers nip at her tires.

Whenever she comes to an obstacle, she jumps over it. The Super MonsterTruck barrels through them.

Atalanta realizes that the Super MonsterTruck is more interested in smashing her than winning the race.

She slams on her brakes. The Super MonsterTruck speeds by her and skids to a halt.

"You're about to be scrap!" the huge beast roars.

Then it charges, tires spinning and engines roaring.

Behind the Super MonsterTruck is the finish line. Atalanta just needs to get by it to win.

The Super MonsterTruck expects her to zig and zag. So Atalanta does something different.

She drives straight at the charging truck! She is small enough to zip right under its axles and finish the race.

CHAPTER 5

MONSTERTRUCK SPEED DASH

The ThunderTrucks gather around to celebrate. Atalanta just won another race! But they are not the only trucks waiting for her at the finish line.

She sees The Boar and the even bigger Atlas. The nine-wheeled Hydra is there, and so is the Cyclops with his one huge headlight.

They are all there to
challenge her to a race.

"Enough is enough!"
Atalanta honks. "One last
race. First one to Royal Rumbler's Decal
Shop is the world speediest truck. Agreed?"

The MonsterTrucks all agree.

"Okay then, to the starting line!"
she honks.

The MonsterTrucks all do as she says.

"Racers, get ready!" the race official

blares

Atalanta revs her engine.

"Get set!"

All the MonsterTrucks rumble and roar.

RUMBLE! RRRR!

"GO!"

Tires spin. Dirt flies. The racers are off!

Atalanta brakes as The Boar veers

left to smash into her. At the same time,

Atlas steers right to ram her. The two

MonsterTrucks crash into each other.

BANG!

Up ahead is Hydra, rumbling along on his nine tires. She zips by him as he tries to run her off the road. Hydra spins out.

Then it is just her and Cyclops. He swerves all over to block her. But Atalanta is too fast. She darts around him. Cyclops turns too sharply and flips over.

Atalanta zooms off.

A little while later, she rolls into the Royal Rumbler's Decal Shop.

"Can I help you?" the Royal Rumbler asks.

Up on the wall is a decal that says "World Speediest Truck."

"I would like that one," Atalanta beeps.

Then she goes outside as all the other trucks show up.

"I was the fastest at the ThunderTruck Super Sprint," Atalanta blares. "I beat Bullistic through the Monster Maze. I won the Endur-X Championship. And I survived the Colossal Course!"

She pauses and beams her brights at the trucks in front of her.

"Are there any other challengers?" Atalanta rumbles.

The MonsterTrucks all turn and sputter away.

Then the ThunderTrucks gather around to congratulate her.

"You are the World's Speediest Truck," Argonutz honks.

"You earned that decal," Hercules beeps.

Atalanta beams brightly. She sure did earn it!

BLAKE HOENA

Blake Hoena grew up in central Wisconsin, where he wrote stories about robots conquering the moon and trolls lumbering around the woods behind his parents' house. He now lives in St. Paul, Minnesota, with his two dogs, Ty and Stich. Blake continues to make up stories about things like space aliens and superheroes, and he has written more than 100 chapter books and graphic novels for children.

FERN CANO

Fernando Cano is an illustrator born in Mexico City, Mexico. He currently resides in Monterrey, Mexico, where he works as a free-lance illustrator and concept artist. He has done illustration work for Marvel, DC Comics, and worked on various video game projects in diverse titles. When he's not making art for comics or books, he enjoys hanging out with friends, singing, rowing, and drawing.